Visions of Valhalla

Visions of Valhalla
A poetic tribute to Richard Wagner

John Davidson

to Wagnerians, past and present

© John Davidson 2016

Illustrations are from the author's collection, unless otherwise credited. Cover image of Wagner by Franz von Lenbach; design by Sarah Bolland. Photo of John Davidson by Matthias Seidenstücker. Production: Laura Vordermayer, with thanks to George Boraman.

A catalogue record for this book is available from the National Library of New Zealand.

ISBN 978-0-947493-30-1

Steele Roberts Publishers
Box 9321 Wellington, Aotearoa New Zealand
info@SteeleRoberts.co.nz • www.SteeleRoberts.co.nz

Contents

Introduction	7
Pilgrims' chorus	13
The year 1813	14
The awakening	15
Die Frist ist um	16
Who else?	17
Cause and effect	18
Musical spark	19
Berlin in 2013	20
Refugees in 2015	22
The ship of Theseus	23
Spare a thought for Minna	24
A dog's life	26
The woman problem	28
Mein Leben	29
Cosima	30
Senta	32
At the Wartburg	34
The wedding march	35
Silence	36
Bridge to worlds beyond	37
The sword	38
Sleep	39
Siegfried at the forge	40
Forest murmurs	41
Then you are Wotan	42
Dragon's blood	44
Trauermusik	45
Wotan's favourite daughter speaks her mind	46
My sixth *Ring*	48
Hier gilt's der Kunst	49

The man with the blue gavotte	50
Parnassus and Paradise	51
The Tristan chord	52
Hunting horns	53
Waiting	54
The wound	55
Parsifal	56
Dresden Amen	57
Thinking about would-be redeemers	58
Richard and Queen Victoria	60
King Ludwig II	61
A tale of two cities	62
In the pink	63
What might have been	64
The millionaire question	65
More than a facelift	66
Once in Bayreuth	68
Wagner and the Greeks	69
What value an opera?	70
Steeplechase	72
The imperfect Wagnerite	73
The jockey club	74
Erlösung dem Erlöser	75
The mind of Wagner	76
What's in a motif?	77
The dream	78
The year 1883	79
NOTES	81

Introduction

The idea for this collection came while I was living for two months in Berlin in 2013, the bicentenary of Richard Wagner's birth. I wrote the first poem at that time after attending the Staatsoper *Ring* cycle. Other poems followed from time to time when I returned to New Zealand, and the collection was largely complete by March this year. It represents a considerable period of reflection on my reading of Wagner scholarship and my experiences of Wagnerian performances. The poems are a mix of the serious and not-so-serious. Most are concerned with aspects of Wagner's life, with individual works or series of works, with his ongoing influence, and with reactions and responses to the man himself and his musical/dramatic legacy. In some cases, a Wagnerian theme is used as a point of entry for thoughts about contemporary issues.

In the 1960s when I was a postgraduate student in London, I became an *habitué* of the Royal Opera House, Covent Garden, and heard my first *Ring* cycle under the baton of Georg Solti. I was also fortunate enough to hear Reginald Goodall conduct Wagner for the English National Opera. These and other performances in those years established a pattern for me which has continued over the subsequent decades, especially in the United Kingdom, Australia, and Germany.

In New Zealand, however, there was for many years no opportunity to see live performances of Wagnerian works, and I had to be content with the occasional concerts involving musical excerpts, while making the most of time spent overseas. All this changed with the ground-breaking production of *Die Meistersinger von Nürnberg* at the International Festival of the Arts in Wellington, in early 1990, when we were at last able to see Donald McIntyre performing Wagner in his home country. Since then there have been further important concerts and a number of notable staged and semi-staged productions featuring McIntyre as well as other New Zealanders of international standing, such as Simon O'Neill and Margaret Medlyn.

The establishment of the still flourishing Wagner Society of New Zealand in 1994 was another milestone for the promotion of the composer's works in this part of the world. A key figure in this has been founding president Heath Lees whose knowledge, musicality, and infectious enthusiasm have been an inspiration to many. Branches of the society now exist in Auckland, Wellington, Christchurch and Dunedin, with regular programmes of lectures, films and other activities.

In the poems, reference is made to some of the key cities and places of residence associated with Wagner. Among these are Leipzig, his birthplace and where he spent his early years, later returning to complete his schooling and have a brief taste of university life. He spent some of his childhood years in Dresden, and the premières of *Rienzi, Der Fliegende Holländer* and *Tannhäuser* were later held there. He had to flee Dresden to avoid arrest after participating in the disastrous revolutionary uprising in 1849. Then there is Riga, which he had been forced to leave in a hurry to escape his creditors in 1839, and Paris. It was in the French capital that he lived hand-to-mouth for more than two years struggling to establish himself as a serious composer, and it was from here in 1861, after another short stay, he retreated in indignation after the disruption of performances of *Tannhäuser* by members of the Jockey Club.

Not overlooked either is Munich (München), where he lived between early 1864 and December 1865 after his 'salvation' by the young, newly crowned king of Bavaria, Ludwig II, before being forced out as a financial liability on the kingdom and a dangerous influence on the king. It was Munich too that saw the premières of *Tristan und Isolde, Die Meistersinger, Das Rheingold* and *Die Walküre*. Venice (Venezia) also features. Wagner was attracted to the city's visual splendour as much as to its flamboyant musical history. After 1876, it more or less became the Wagner family's second home and it was there he was to die in 1883. Although not mentioned, Zurich, where he settled in 1849 after the escape into exile from Dresden, is also very much in the background to several poems. Specific reference is, however, made to the *Asyl* (asylum), the residence adjoining Otto Wesendonck's villa in a Zurich suburb, put at Wagner's disposal by his benefactor. Wagner lived here between 1857 and 1858.

Tribschen, the house on Lake Lucerne which Wagner made his home in 1866, does not appear as such in any poem, but the performance there of the *Siegfried Idyll* to celebrate Cosima's birthday on Christmas Day 1870 does. Perhaps the most famous residence associated with Wagner today, however, is Wahnfried, the house in Bayreuth into which he and Cosima moved in 1874, and in the garden of which they are buried. A specific reference is made to this. Bayreuth itself looms large, as the town where Wagner was able to establish the *Festspielhaus* as the venue for the first performances of the complete *Ring* cycle and also *Parsifal*. The tradition of a festival of Wagnerian works in Bayreuth remains to this day.

Wagner is nothing if not a polarising figure, and his musical compositions are likewise objects of ongoing controversy. On the personal side, his relationship with his first wife, the singer Minna Planer, was fraught from the start. The circumstances leading to his second marriage (to the daughter of Franz Liszt, Cosima, who was married to Hans von Bülow, a great admirer of Wagner and champion of his works), is well known and caused a scandal. His infatuation with Mathilde Wesendonck (who was at least part of the inspiration for *Tristan und Isolde*, and five of whose poems he set to music to produce the song cycle known as the *Wesendonck Lieder*) is still the subject of much speculation, while his flings with various other women add further spice to the subject. Then there is his inability to live within his means, his penchant for silks and other luxuries, and his constant trouble with creditors, not to mention the extraordinary affection felt for him by King Ludwig II and the financial support lavished on him from that source.

If that isn't enough, there are the works. Wagner always had those who believed in what he was doing musically and those who ridiculed him. In the former category were Liszt (who conducted the première of *Lohengrin* in Weimar while Wagner was in exile), von Bülow and Bruckner. But some of his detractors characterised his music as cacophony. *Tristan und Isolde* was received rapturously by some, including Nietzsche who considered it a masterpiece even after his celebrated falling-out with its composer. On the other hand, no less an artist than Clara Schumann found it 'repugnant'. The storm of words about Wagner's music in general continues to rage today, as devotees cross swords with those who write off anything Wagnerian as loud, drawn-out and boring. And there are similarly varied responses to Wagner's prose writings as well as his libretti for the operas. Wagner himself displayed a range of attitudes to the work of other composers, not hesitating to debunk practitioners of contemporary operatic traditions he was aiming to supersede. Hence his criticisms of much, though not all, of French and Italian music.

Another vexing matter is Wagner's attitude to the Jewish question, as seen among other contexts in his 1850 tract *Das Judenthum in der Musik* (Jewishness in music). While he and some other family members have been tarred with an anti-Semitic brush, he has also been condemned by association with Nazism, given that Hitler was such an admirer of his work and often visited Bayreuth, befriending Winifred, widow of Wagner's son Siegfried, and their sons Wieland and Wolfgang. The entire Bayreuth phenomenon fell under a cloud as a result, and for some that cloud will never entirely lift. In addition, the Wagner family has become synonymous with rivalries and in-fighting, and the battle for control of Bayreuth has had a negative effect on Wagner's own reputation.

With regard to the operas today, the focus of most controversy is on 'modern' productions, many of which have become exemplars of director-driven *Regietheater*. They have infuriated traditionalists who yearn to see something approaching productions as Wagner himself conceived and implemented them, but have been welcomed by others.

Rising above all this, however, is the music, celebrated by traditionalist and avant-garde Wagnerians alike. Underpinning the entire Wagnerian phenomenon too is an extraordinary range of scholarship, with ongoing debate about most aspects of Wagner's career, and a proliferation of interpretations of the works which employ all the resources of contemporary literary and psychological theories. There seems to be no let-up in the fascination Wagner has exerted on so many minds and hearts.

As the poems in this collection contain a large number of allusions to aspects of Wagner's life and to responses to the man and his work, there are some explanatory notes at the back. Further information, especially about the operas, can be extracted from the various libretti or summaries of the plots, as well as from books about Wagner and his life. It's rewarding research.

The illustrations are from a variety of sources. When attending the Festspiele I have always written home, ensuring I had the distinctive postmark on the stamps. Because of my interest in philately I have included images of stamps relevant to the theme of the collection (the poem on page 70 refers to some of these).

I would like to acknowledge the part played by my Wagnerian friends, especially those in New Zealand and Australia, as my knowledge and appreciation of Wagner developed over the years. I am also most grateful to Heath Lees, Barry Millington and Janet Davidson for their encouragement of this project, as well as to Matthias Seidenstücker for providing photographs of the Berlin monument under renovation, the bust of Cosima and the grave of the dog Russ. The editorial and production assistance of Laura Vordermayer has been invaluable. My deepest debt of gratitude is to my wife Brigitte, who has been unfailingly loyal during my obsession.

John Davidson
Wellington

Pilgrims' chorus

after act 1, scene 3 of Tannhäuser

Zu dir wall ich, mein Festspielhaus,
das du des Pilgers Hoffnung bist.
Be praised, Bayreuth, sweet and pure.
To our Pilgrimage, please be gracious
(and by the way, we would have liked some tickets).

The year 1813

In the year he was born the first pineapples were planted in Hawai'i, the 'war of 1812' became a misnomer in North America and Simon Bolivar was proclaimed *El Libertados* in the South. Campaigning Napoleon gained the upper hand until the Battle of the Nations near Leipzig (no less) put an end to all that — in the meantime anyway — while the Peninsula War clouds were fast approaching French soil. *Pride and Prejudice* had left an impression on polite drawing room sofas, its title hinting prophetically. European explorers were now pushing westward from Sydney, and Søren Kierkegaard saw the light of existence too. After the Leipzig birth came those of Verdi and Georg Büchner, and Beethoven's seventh symphony deafened its first concert hall.

But nothing could compare with the 22nd of May.

The awakening

Solti's bobbing energy was
my initiation as I sat in awe
among seasoned acolytes.
This was extending the limits
of the imaginable.

I floated through the crush
bar at intervals, straining
my ears to catch splinters
of wisdom flying pointedly
from wine glasses.

Lifetimes of service around
the shrine haunted seats,
stairs, carpets, crush bars.
Programme sellers guarded
treasuries of enticement.

Walking back to my hotel
through Covent Garden's
dining streets after this
awakening I savoured
the screaming in my skull.

Die Frist ist um

It doesn't need a Klingsor
or expectant Holländer
to make such pronouncements.

It's always time, in London,
Seattle, Bayreuth
or distant Wellington —

for the depths of the Rhine
to be dazzled with gold,
for storm and flight,
for the antics of a boyish
hero, the love and leave-
taking of a marginally
maturer one, the frosty
contiguity of passion,
dungeon of delights,
trial of an innocent,
the final landlocking
of seven years, admonition
of a grey-beard knight,
betrothal to an unknown
quantity —

even an attempted abduction
and Roman factionalism.
It's always time.

Who else?

Who else could have seen *Lohengrin*
as the final stretch of a drying watercourse?
Who else could have paused to articulate
a new vision while sensing its cadences
already stirring in the undergrowth
of his intuition? Who else could have pulled
the darkest emotions into daylight
and laid bare the yearnings of humanity's soul?

Who else could have survived deprivation,
prejudice and raw hostility locking horns
with idolisation? Who else, as composer,
could have transformed the very identities
of kings and philosophers? Who else too
could have seized entire art forms to direct them
through signposts of his own devising?

Who else could have seethed so in spirit
in the imagination of decades to follow?
Who else?

Cause and effect

There are times when you wonder
if you've just been taken for a ride,
if a warlock has hoodwinked you,
wrested control of your reasoning,
coaxed your emotive life through
latitudes whose breath has caressed you
before drying your reservoir of
resistance,

when you battle to understand why
you've allowed this, why you seem
to have lost touch with earth and air
and the marketplaces of normality
in those perilous hours of surrender,
and whether those experiences
you believe you've had ever really
happened.

And so you pluck at the desultory
strings of white and then black
and forward and backward
until you hear again this other music
that encroaches on respectability,
that deconstructs certainties,
and spirits you away to exhilaration's
Valhalla.

Musical spark

Beethoven unconsciously
stumbled into Loge's role,

sending a spark that would
flicker in undergrowth

before forcing a trail
to daylight, then seizing

the latent fuel source
of an awakening world

to end as an inferno consuming
effigies of Weber, Marschner

Bellini, Meyerbeer, even
Berlioz, with tongues

of *Freude, Freude* in darting
interplay with *Leiden, Leiden,*

scorching and purifying
before sinking down

to eternal preservation
in the garden of Wahnfried.

Berlin in 2013

Richard ist Leipziger,
which is true enough and
apt for a marketing ploy.

Meanwhile Dresden claims
to have put him in upper case
while here in Berlin
the Valkyries are riding
and the Dutchman flying.

Nothing like a bicentenary.
Put a ring around this year
and steal the thunder
from Bayreuth's cloud cover.

Press the thumbs, though,
against potential disruption
from Ver.di.

'The Dutchman is flying'.
The Great Operas by J. Cuthbert Hadden

Refugees in 2015

There's an irony here —
elements in Leipzig,
birthplace of the Master,
campaigned to obliterate
the memory of his presence
in Richard-Wagner-Platz,
renaming it in solidarity
as Refugees-Welcome-Platz.

The carriageways of the mind
echo with the sound of hooves
scampering away from Riga
or in even greater danger later
from Dresden's ruin towards
the sanctuary of Switzerland.
There at least was a welcome
and the chance to change
the very face of music.

Refugees can sometimes repay
with interest those who take
them in. At some point, though,
the cost may become too great.

The ship of Theseus

The Wartburg may be dressed as a recycling plant
and nobility may metamorphose into vermin.
Mountain sides may find themselves gas stations
and motels, or Nibelheim a rogue laboratory.
Castle stronghold may replicate company office
and the deepest wisdom of Earth herself may
be summoned from a library's basement stacks.
An aspiring Mastersinger may play Jackson
Pollock and you may get rotting rabbits for doves.

In such a world, even if the music is sacrosanct,
the question is whether it remains Wagner.

Minna Planer (in 1853) with her dog Peps.
Watercolour by Clementine Stockar-Escher.

Spare a thought for Minna

Talented in her own right
and by all accounts beautiful, she spotted
something in the new conductor
of the Magdeburg company, while he
responded fully to her sensuality.
But it was not a smart move to marry
a man with growing experience of evading
creditors. She would have been better
advised to cling to her lover rather
than hightailing it to Riga to be welcomed
by a connoisseur of extravagance.

Family rivalry next, flight mode where
a seatbelt might have come in handy, illicit
border crossing, sickening voyage, dragged
from milepost to gas lamp, ending up
in impecunious Paris, losing jewellery,
clothes, wedding ring even in return
for pawn tickets later onsold. Her talent

was now reduced to the composition
of begging letters to save the genius
from a debtors' prison. Always the gnawing
worry about mere survival as the debtor
himself agonised over lack of recognition
and the frustration of his artistic dreams.

Dresden may have promised much more,
but her name was then even dropped
from the flying libretto for Senta
as her husband's foothold in the fantasy world
of opera strengthened. Then he went
and played the revolutionary guard
and that became the abrupt goodnight
to Saxony. Why did she join him
in Zurich? They were never suited
to each other. He didn't want her;
he told her so. Jessie had been more appealing,
and she was to stand no chance with waltzing
Mathilde. There was just the ignominy
of pleading political pardon for him,
heart condition and nervous exhaustion,
becoming merely his housekeeper, later,
his refusal to rejoin her in Dresden, just a visit
to make token provision and sever
the final slender strand. She was never again
to see that husband of hers. He had now
rectangulated with von Bülow, Cosima
and his fancy young king, and had changed
the course of Western music. Then she died.

There's the final irony that her grave rests
close to those of the original Tristan and Isolde.

A dog's life

It was an unusual household
he joined, manic master,
long-suffering mistress. Soon
on the move in a crowded coach,
border crossing, embarkation.

Had he known what lay ahead,
would he ever have loped up
the gangway? Imagine him barking
dolefully as the *Thetis* rolled
like a toy amid flying waves,
his energies fully channelled
into raw aggression against intruders
in the cabin, sensing those scheduled
days turning into weeks that,
unbeknown to him, fed his
master's mind with myth and music.

Imagine him again in Soho
and before he might recover
his equipoise in Boulogne and then
in Paris. But his troubles were just
beginning, as the sustenance
required for that substantial frame
was simply not forthcoming.

Was it any wonder he took French leave,
or some time later in the street,
when he heard the penniless call,
turned tail and disappeared
into the shadows? This was Robber,
but his former master's pen ensured
his name has long outlived him.

'*Hier ruht und wacht Wagners Russ*' — here
Wagner's Russ rests and keeps watch. This dog
of Wagner's is buried close to his master's grave
in the Wahnfried garden.
Matthias Seidenstücker

The woman problem

Creative artists seem to be given a longer lead
when it comes to personal behaviour, especially
of a sexual nature, and Wagner was a romantic
hero of the 19th century. What would you expect?
In any case, he and Minna were incompatible,
their marriage was a sham and, don't forget,
she'd had more than one fling herself early on
and a daughter called *Schwester* to show for it.
Mathilde's Otto was an odd being who raked
in the shekels of kudos from hosting the famous
composer, and Wagner needed a smiling muse,
while she probably kept him at Lieder's length
anyway. Then there was von Bülow. Well, he
was a bully, and bullies deserve what they get
and there's no sympathy later when they play
hangdog. Jessie comes to mind too, but here
the Master was 'between relationships' and
the elopement plans did crumble. Judith was
a dabble and was herself a practised dabbler,
and the King of Bayreuth deserved a little extra.
We can forgive and forget too the other trivial
skirt-chasing episodes because testosterone
demands its pound of flesh. On the other hand,
there are the prudes who castigate, but they're just
envious and 'true love' has always greeted them
with the Catullan finger. Even Father Franz
gave the okay to a marriage.

Mein Leben

Yes, well, a masterful exercise
in self-promotion
and the construction of a life
as seen from the bars
of one mind's prison,
a storied life whose termination
was a new beginning for silk
and velvet and a Festspielhaus
to rival castles in the air.

Cosima

The Brown Book was one gift to him,
devotion another, a posthumous life
in Bayreuth the lasting third. Was there
also a perfect fourth? We could mention
that marriage of minds to which
she added the patience to absorb, edit,
and reproduce his articulate streams
of consciousness.

His gifts to her were the *Siegfried Idyll*,
a cast list of children and enhancement
of her inherited status as the daughter
of virtuosity. If we probe further we may
discover in later years a tyrant reflecting
certain tyrannies of her upbringing
and downloading the harsh lessons
of guilt and suffering.

And she had the nose
to sniff out competition.

Cosima, sculpted by Arno Breker, in the gardens of the Festspielhaus, Bayreuth.
Matthias Seidenstücker

Senta

He bursts out of the picture frame
through storm clouds, offering a treasury
of avarice to the calculating father,
but treasure of another kind to the daughter,
the spinner of imaginings.

Previous attachments now seem nothing
to her, as she feels angel wings forming
and the glow of mission burning her eyes.

But she fails to appreciate the implications
of the truth that what is infernal
will remain infernal, and the seductive sails
of story will be lowered as the love ship
vanishes forever beneath the waves.

The Dutchman rising heavenwards.
The Great Operas by J. Cuthbert Hadden.

At the Wartburg

Greenery materialising
before disbelieving eyes
from the womb that nurtures
seeds of absolution.

It may appear too late
to save this life
of tortured contradiction

but it has the final word
against the childless
womb of Venus.

The wedding march

There was a time when the bride
negotiating the optimistic aisle
was assured of many years, often
a lifetime of partnership, even
if betrayal and brutality did unlock
the bedroom door with a skeleton
key on more than one occasion.

In our day, if it gets as far
as marriage, that same negotiation
of the aisle spurred by the musical
legacy of Wagner so often echoes
the prelude to Elsa's perilous
flirtation with happiness
before the uncoupling
of the contract
and everlasting
separation.

Silence

Silence precedes the deep E-flat.
It exists before the prelude
to the beginning, which will slowly
grow to unfold the prelude
to everything. But the germination
has dwelt in the silence
the E-flat shatters,
to nurture ripples swelling
into waves. Creation shines through
these waters that carry the golden seeds
of corruption.

Bridge to worlds beyond

The rainbow bridge whose crossing
Wagner orchestrated for Wotan,
with his family all agog, extends
far beyond the giant battlements
of Valhalla —

to the womb of earth, to an empty wolf skin
on the forest floor, to a ruffian's hut
and the wedding gift of an embedded sword,

then on to destiny's battleground,
a mountain rock and ring of fire,
the riddling hut within another forest,
resting place for the wanderer,

mouth of a dragon's cave, and back
to that Valhalla now condemned to flames,

further also for Wagner
himself at least — to a love
that's consummated

through darkness, a prize song
and the reanimated ceremony
of the Grail,

even beyond these worlds
to death throes in Venice
and a quickening legacy.

Donner accomplished much more
than he ever imagined
with his booming
necromancy.

The sword

The sword is waiting for us to discover,
often in a time of crisis. We will not
be alone at that hour, but the strength
of another arm will assist us as we slip
the iron from its accommodating tree.

This sword will then accompany
our flight from reality, and fatal encounter
with destiny, its fragments to be carried
into a wilderness and forged again
by a new generation created now
to shatter blocking spears, dismantle
fearsome shadows, even reach to peaks
that we could never scale, but which
in course of time will be engulfed
in a panoply of blazing twilight.

Sleep

When we are sleeping on the rock,
when our eyelids have been coaxed
into closure, when the mount
with whom we used to ride adventure
is comatose too, we become oblivious
to the stormclouds massing outside
the ring of fire surrounding us.

The moisture in these clouds
can be poisonous, and rain down
poverty, homelessness, hunger, betrayal,
corporate greed, digital surveillance,
information overload, environ-
mental pollution, malice, murder
and the virus of malpractice.

Our vulnerability covered only
by a breastplate can then be exposed
by a single kiss.

Siegfried at the forge

He can bluster and shout
but he can't exactly sing,
and you know that by the time
he's supposed to be romantically
engaged with a resurgent Brünnhilde
he'll be braying like a donkey (if he
doesn't actually lose his voice),
and thrusting a numbing blade
through what should be sensual.

And if you're unlucky
she'll be strident as well
and you'll want to block your ears
and pray that he'll be replaced
for the twilight of the gods
which, if he's still there, may be
not so much a twilight as a total darkness
amid your rapidly disintegrating sanity.

Frida Leider
as Brünnhilde
in *Die Walküre*.
from *Opera at Home*,
The Gramophone Co, 1925

Forest murmurs

There are whisperings that haunt
youth in moments of solitude

when questions of origin begin
to pinprick the expanding mind.

They form a rustling curtain
behind a showpiece of birdsong

as yet not able to be interpreted.
A rough reed pipe fails to mimic

this song, but a horn awakens
the dragon, whose bright blood,

once tasted, will unlock meaning
from the song and lead on towards

an adulthood where innocence
will dissolve, and forest murmurs

yield to wild beatings of the heart.

Then you are Wotan

When you carve agreements in wood
that your own disregard erases,
when you sublimate your affection
to reach for the lustre of power

when you blindly trust the security
of heights and defensive stonework,
and seek allies stemming from
the mystery of the earth's deepest core

when you initiate your very issue
into the ways of marauding wolves
and bury your designs so teasingly
in the tight darkness of tree trunks

when you manipulate the desperate
into paths increasingly desperate
and organise for them the licence
to cross beyond sanctity's border

when the threads of your skulduggery
are unpicked in one haughty gesture
and all you can do is capitulate
and passionately prefigure the end,

when you are forced to unleash
the death spasm of a cherished agent
and then pursue through storm clouds
the disobedience you never anticipated

when you doom what most touches
you to lose inherited privileges and
lie asleep to you for ever, as you
surround her with mournful fire

when you condemn yourself to wander
the riddling world as a shadow
in forest corners, observing but never
acting, your influence obliterated

when your final energies are splintered
beside the threshold of earth's wisdom,
when you must stand and oversee
the fuelling of your own immolation.

Then you are tragic.
Then you are Wotan.

Anton van Roy as Wotan in *Das Rheingold*.
from *Opera at Home*, The Gramophone Co, 1925

Dragon's blood

Spilling the dragon's blood
requires fearlessness; tasting it
gives you the advantage
over the other enemy, the dark
scheming that likewise works
to contrive your demise and reap
the benefits of heroism.

Having tasted blood, you can read
thoughts, cold ambitions, dreams
of power, treachery. And you have
no scruples either about dealing
the fatal blow to years of false intimacy.

And it's the same taste of blood
can guide your puppet strings
through singing forests, past decaying
barriers, to peaks of discovery
and reckless abandon, when you can
step through fire as though it were cobweb.

But later, even as you sound the horn
with its deceptive aura of invincibility,
you succumb so easily to snares
laid by sharper minds, cruel, brooding
and poisonous, and you come to learn
that even the dragon's blood
can never help you.

Trauermusik

This is the music that follows us all
to our marriage with earth or ash,
its impulsive, brassy notes disguised
as tears.

Through the minds of our entourage
motifs manipulate their passageway.
We may have enticed dragons from
their lairs,

and toyed with their menace,
unsheathing stabbing words before
dispatching them with casual scorn
to darkness.

We may have forged clean contracts
with kindred and with foreign blood.
We may also have betrayed fidelity
through ignorance,

or forgetfulness, or through designs
of those seeking to deprive us of our
inheritance in the cause of their own
avaricious worlds.

And yet as the music surges and dies
there may be more than one who
will be striving to own our spirit
for eternity.

Wotan's favourite daughter speaks her mind

I preferred the first ending ...

For a start, I would have been allowed
to perform a really useful service. What
a weakling, by the way, my father was,
as he gave new meaning to the kiss
of death, and he never learned to curb
his temper either. I liked the idea of final
freedom and floating up to Valhalla
with Siegfried; I would have paid
due respect to *Allvater*.

With *Herrlicher du* on my lips
I would have hidden what I really thought
of him. Eternal, guilt-free happiness
for all. Just the ticket. But then *he*
stuffed it all up through *his* inability
to keep things succinct, and decided
that *he* needed a prequel to *Siegfried's Tod*
and dreamed up *Der Junge Siegfried*.
And then *he* came up with the idea
of a prequel to the prequel and I found
myself in it up to my neck early on —
not that I minded the attention, of course,
and as it turned out I did love *Hojotoho!
Hojotoho! Heiaha! Heiaha! Hojotoho! Heiaha!*
But by the time *he* was finally satisfied, with
a prelude to his prequel as well, the result
was that *he* had to do some editing
and make changes and tilt the balance
so that my father became central and *he*
dragged in the violation and withering

of the ash tree, which demanded its felling
and fuel for Valhalla's inferno which meant
a different destiny for me.

So now instead of bearing my hero aloft
to bliss I was to be incinerated along with him,
toss the firebrand to ignite Valhalla and bring
an end to the gods themselves. At least this
meant that I'd go out in a blaze of glory,
and that's the way my adoring fans know it —
so I can be thankful at least for that. But *he*
then had to read Schopenhauer (and pretend
he'd anticipated him), which meant *he* devised
words which have become ingrained in my
long-suffering spirit, even if *he* never set them
to music for me to sing — at least *he* spared me
that. But *he* really wanted me to see
the world itself end and evaporate
into an eternal nothingness without desire
and illusion, with the lament: *Trauernder
Liebe tiefstes Leiden schloss die Augen mir auf:
enden sah ich die Welt.* At least, as I say, I was
spared having to project these words into the
breathless darkness of unnumbered auditoria.

It's painful enough as it is!

My sixth *Ring*

At the pre-performance drinkies
it was all a question of how many —
how many *Rings*, I mean, had one attended.

I was in a reasonable comfort zone
since this was my sixth (including
three at Bayreuth) and so I commanded
some status with third or fourth Ringers,
for example, even more so with those
who confessed with blushes to be *Ring* virgins.

But there were plenty with teens or twenties
or thirties under their belts who ambled
with easy arrogance from huddle to huddle
flaunting their superiority.

Even they, however, kowtowed to the woman
at her fifty-first who took it all as matter
of fact. And there were dark whispers
about 'someone we know' who'd broken
the century mark. That divine being wasn't
there but if s/he had been there's no doubt
that mass *proskynesis* would have threatened
the viability of the carpet fibre.

For all the carry-on, however, the one
useful comment? *Make the most of this Ring.*
It may be your last.

Hier gilt's der Kunst

It's questionable if art can ever
be seen as the priority. Politics
always seems to slip in its credentials,
even if these are disguised as the politics
encompassing art. Then there's personal
ambition, sometimes a mask for avarice
itself, and there's also the imperative
of an attraction that may be love,
or love's second cousin, lust.

Put the microscope on Walther, Eva,
Pogner, the circus clown Beckmesser,
the Mastersingers *en masse* as a solid
phalanx of propriety, even add in Sachs,
the tortured 'also ran'. Where is the priority
centred? And invariably lurking just beneath,
to rise as tiger from the knotted undergrowth
is our symbiotic *Wahn*. Wagner knew this.

The man with the blue gavotte

long after Wallace Stevens

The man bent his head to the ground,
A dancer of sorts. The town was Nürnberg.

They said, 'You perform a blue gavotte,
You do not number steps as they are.'

The man replied, 'Steps as they are
Are changed in the blue gavotte.'

And they said then, 'But dance, you must,
A figure beyond us, yet ourselves,

A figure in the blue gavotte
Of a world exactly as it should be.'

Parnassus and Paradise

The poet Walther began his quest
in morning light that harboured roses.
A garden was enticing him through
a curtain of air and sweet blossom
towards a tree shading a vision
of Eve in Paradise.

Twilight wrapped around his pathway
of dreams upwards to a spring of pure water
beneath a laurel bush, with the starlight
filtered through its leaves, and baptism
by the Muse of Parnassus.

The waking day revealed to him his fantasy
embodied as woman merging Parnassus
and Paradise into a unity of the earth's
most treasured artifact of perfection,
won as the prize of song.

Fleeting moment of exhilaration for Walther,
that would so soon spiral downwards to reality
for his other audience in the verses
of a shoe-maker's admonitory epilogue.

The Tristan chord

It is familiar yet
ever a new experience
as it floats its discordant harmony

and evokes the clash
of waves, wrathful pride
and pre-occupation, prefiguring

the yearning that
breaks against castle walls
and seeks to imbibe oblivion,

the impetuous embrace
of darkness, bewilderment
at dignity betrayed, the tortures

of wound and waiting,
death without reunion, and last,
the outpouring into bleak emptiness.

It is familiar, yet
of ever unremembered power.

Hunting horns

Imagination transforms them
into leaves rustling in the wind
and a fountain's flutter.

Desire burns more keenly
than the torch and strives
to seize and extinguish it.

Warnings of malevolence
will fall on ears attuned only
to a friendship false, while

short minutes of expectation
appear as hours of wasteful
procrastination.

Caution's conscience is abruptly
dismissed to the heights
of a watch tower, and

all that matters now is night
and the embracing amplitude
of infidelity,

an infidelity changed into
a faithfulness to over-
ride boundaries.

Ecstasy, too, thrusts a canopy
of protective foliage over
blinded senses …

But those hunting horns
will soon return to clash
with Love's harmony.

Frau Minne must expose
her throbbing breast
to the sword.

Waiting

I live just to see her again,
but she doesn't come.
Nothing to be heard except
the plangent note of the cor anglais

intoned by a shepherd,
and occasional whispers
of comfort that inveigle
my sleep or wakeful delirium.

No report of ship
to signal joy from the masthead.
Nothing to relieve pain
splitting the atoms of body and heart.

The beckoning finger
of darkness that vibrated
with substance when we embraced
in the garden so long ago

is skeletal in her absence.
If she does ever come
she will unbandage wounds
inflicted by our lacerated destinies.

The wound

The wound springs from an enticing source
that promises a flowering of the senses
but suddenly enervates and condemns
to a lonely couch of introspection
and longing for the silence of release.

Energies that should radiate
to every encircling limb
shrivel inside a contracting hub,
as the wheel's spin clogs.

It's only the instrument serving
the trauma's source that can bring
a redemption, lodged in another
saving hand.

Parsifal

We all shoot the swan in youthful
trespass ignorant of our misdeed.
Not all of us, though, get off
so lightly and get a second chance

to be embraced as saviour fool.
And the second chance, if it comes
at all, is first a hesitant welcome
home after years of wandering

through the doubts and blood
of blandishments and bad Fridays.
There is still the defining kiss
to encounter and break free from,

and the flying spear to grasp
before it can strike its numbing blow.
That would again demand
an abdication from the power

to rule and radiate healing light.
And who else would then complete
the holy circle's circumference
and care for Kundry?

Dresden Amen

The jury's still out about
his dedication to the Dresden uprising,
as a babble of voices continues
to prosecute and defend.

Red-handed guilt swept
under the censor's carpet.

No. Only ever at the fringes.

Exaggerated his own importance
(need I say) while editing out
significant contribution.

Real target just the musical establishment.

Serious charges on the arrest warrant.

Hearsay evidence only.

Presence in the Kreuzkirche tower
as direct an involvement as
being on the barricades.

Just spent the time philosophising.

At all events the authorities
were keen to put the clamps
on him, so flight and exile
was his only viable option,
and barring a slice of luck
he would have suffered
the fate of Röckel and Bakunin.
In the end, however you view it,
the only productive towers
he was to climb were musical
and dramatic ones.

Thinking about would-be redeemers

The leap from a cliff was designed
to lay a legend to rest, or perhaps
it was that Senta scrambled
up the staircase of her mind
and found no way out.

The branch may have sprouted
to set the seal on Elisabeth's self-
sacrifice, but would an eternity
minus carnal self-indulgence
have been bliss for Tannhäuser?

The champion from a distant land
put his redeemer's stake
emphatically in the ground
but imposed tricky conditions
and only saved an enchanted swan.

Brangäne foolishly thought
that by playing with potions
she was saving two lives, but at least
she saved an opera which otherwise
would have expired in the first act.

Walther appeared to rescue Eva
from an imagined loveless marriage,
and with the help of some creativity
at the last may well have saved
the Mastersingers from atrophy.

Kundry's herbs from Arabia
could never assuage Amfortas' pain
as a sacred spear supposedly could,
and it was no innocent fool
who cradled Richard's dying moments.

Göta Ljungberg as Elisabeth in *Tannhäuser*.
Opera at Home, London: The Gramophone Co. 1925.

Richard and Queen Victoria

Foggy London town was never exactly
one of his preferred stomping grounds
but he did meet the Queen after a spell
of energised conducting in the service

of music (and money). He was tickled
pink (so to speak) about his embrace
by the very highest echelons of English
society when he was *persona non grata*

in German territory and not a favourite,
so it appeared, with the French either,
not to mention wolf hounds of the Press.
Meanwhile, she'd taken a shine to the

Tannhäuser overture, even if she found
unorthodox tempi in his treatment
of the Classics as she'd been acquainted
with them at the time. So imagine them

eyeball-to-eyeball in the interval
with the Prince Consort and a plethora
of hangers-on, scribbling mental notes
to be translated later into writing.

Appearances can be most deceptive too.
She grossly underestimated his age,
while taking in his low height, prominent
forehead and hooked nose. For his own

part he observed friendliness if lack
of stature, along with a reddish nose,
and distinct absence of feminine allure.
We are amused.

King Ludwig II

The waters of Lake Starnberg hide mysteries
of why, and what his last thoughts were, but

there was mystery enough before that, why
their stars crossed as they did, and why his

boyish vulnerability became the instrument
for the birthing of Valhalla and Monsalvat.

Was his accession to the throne good fortune
or misfortune — for himself, for Bavaria?

What would he have done without his position
and feathered obsessions? What would his idol

have done without him? And was his deception
by the Cosima subterfuge really the willing

self-deception of a diseased mind? In the end,
should we just be eternally grateful to him?

A tale of two cities

Venezia shapes the *Tristan* tryst,
and sound bites of a soul score his diary,
once he's shaken the *Asyl*'s dust
from his sandals.

Venezia again plays genial host to a lion
licking his wounds from the Parisian mauling
while Eva and Walther exercise his brain
and the Wesendoncks his heart.

München beckons later: first base a lodging
by lake and castle, then a second base
of luxury living, one Isolde to be born,
another to stretch to the stratosphere (when
she recovers her voice) and *Das Leben* springs
to life. München, though, gives him
his marching orders, but he can return
for the Nürnberg triumph, and it premières
a (reluctant) *Rheingold* and Wotan's
fatal humiliation.

More than a decade passes and it's Venezia
he reaches when on Italian soil again
with his heart malfunctioning. It's to Venezia
he retires after the energies of *Parsifal*
are spent, where a flower maiden is said
to have raised the level of passion in the palace.

At all events, this tale of two cities
ends abruptly in a funereal gondola.

In the pink

This is how he left the world,
as he'd been while part of it.

He'd come to drape his body,
as his private rooms were also

draped, and as his dreams were
curtained. Perfumes gave him

the highs that others sought
to self-inflict through stupefying

substances. His luxury became
iconic, praised and pilloried,

the tangible reward of royalty.
Although the fashions of Paris

have long since faded and cracked,
the silk still breathes in the music.

What might have been

Barbarossa might have been resurrected
from his sleep in the mountains to ride
as champion against the stifling church,
and inaugurate a people's utopia sated
with the blessings of artistic freedom.

If not that, then Jesus of Nazareth might
have arisen from the Gospels' grip
to shake the dust from divine sandals,
overturn the capitalist changing tables,
and raise free love over legal contracts.

Achilles was another option, destined
to bestride a new world as superhuman
and rinse away all contaminating stains
from the waters of the immortal Styx.

Wieland der Schmied was even more
promising, with wings crafted to trump
swords forged under duress and ensure
an escape with beloved Schwanhilde.

Wagner himself would have been borne
aloft in triumph with the German *Volk*
released from royal slavery's ignominy.

In the end, though, such melodies
were subsumed in the ringing motifs
of the dragon slayer who alas was ultimately
doomed to stumble in the pathways
to his over-optimistic vision of glory.

The millionaire question

'Who wants to be a millionaire?'
I do. That is, if it would mean
among other things acquiring
one of those boxes at the Met.

And if I did, you could be sure
that I'd never sleep through
Wagner. No. I'd be wide awake
and usually in a state of ecstasy,

surfing pleasure waves on a board
of well-heightened wakefulness.
'Who wants to be a millionaire?'
Indeed! If you put that question

to me, Frank Sinatra, you'd get
a very different response and an
on-the-spot and enthusiastic
application to join High Society.

More than a facelift

He rests on a perch aloft, disdainful,
statuesque, yet now forlorn at the edge
of the Tiergarten, the elements' rage
obliging an acrylic glass canopy
over his head. Wolfram draws his attention
to renovation gear disfiguring the base,
indignantly upstaging Brünnhilde
as a mournful Niobe clone and grovelling
Tannhäuser, all three frozen in time
along with Alberich who embraces
the ephemeral fruits of love forsworn.

Life is here in short supply. To find
more hint of it, cut right across town
to von Werner's painting of the memorial's
unveiling, complete with its colours and
thronging ceremony, though not everyone
is paying much attention there either.
But back at the statue there will soon be
new noses for composer and his creature
Minnesinger, not to mention some fingers,
toes, wisps of beard, and buttocks.

"It's all Brünnhilde's fault," Wolfram seems to be saying. This statue of Wagner by Gustav Eberlein was unveiled in Berlin in 1903, twenty years after the composer's death. The photo shows it in 2016, being cleaned and renovated.
Matthias Seidenstücker

Once in Bayreuth

Once in Bayreuth the *Hakenkreuz*
manoeuvred its crooked march
through the streets, and memories
became encrusted with its banners
of death. Battle lines were drawn
and the *Markgräfliches Opernhaus*
was almost caught in the crossfire.

Instead, it saved the synagogue —
from burning, at least. Shrines
that pilgrims decorate religiously
with their emotions were flecked
with pollution, and name, text,
score and song highlighted
with venom. Today we ponder
the irony of cleansing bombs.

Wagner and the Greeks

There were lessons to be learned
from the ancient Athenian example,
of an idealised community
along with a *Gesamtkunstwerk*
springing directly from the people.

Aeschylus was the model conceived
as somehow unspoiled, with raw yet
vibrant *melopoiia*, dance and *poiesis*,
the decline beginning even with polished
Sophocles, and you could simply write
Euripides off with his intellectualising.

So Aeschylus it was and a society
that represented itself, to itself,
in a primal setting of light and beauty.
German art, 'The Artwork of the Future',
could emulate this and re-programme Europe
with the shutdown of Gallic artificiality.

What was sadly overlooked, however,
was the fact the Athenians also
practised ostracism. Even in ancient
Athens envy stalked the colonnades
just as enmity would poison opera houses,
coffee shops, and palace corridors.

What value an opera?

In January 1933 a new chancellor shows his face
to the people. Later that same year, whether by
design or coincidence, the German post office
issues its annual stamp set for Deutsche Nothilfe,
celebrating works of his favourite composer.

First off the printing block is a brown Tannhäuser
with lyre, at 3 + 2 Reichspfennige. A dark blue
Holländer clings to the rigging at 4 + 2, and light
green Rhine daughters tease the Nibelung
for 5 + 2. Hans Sachs bends dark green over the last

at 6 + 4, and Siegfried in clear orange at 8 + 4
removes breastplate from the supine Valkyrie,
proceeding to demolish the dragon in crimson
at 12 + 3. The lovers clasp the potion's cup
in turquoise at 20 + 10 (the stakes are rising),

swan and sword flank Lohengrin coloured in
violet ultramarine at 25 + 15, the climax being
the dark lilac Parsifal raising the Holy Grail
at 40 + 35 Reichspfennige. Nine stamps of value
but with one significant canonical omission.

Legend has it, though, that *Götterdämmerung*
received its fullest value in May 1945
when even the bunker was crumbling.

Steeplechase

Leading was Aeschylus, then came Shakespeare with Wagner following gamely well behind. Or perhaps Shakespeare had taken front running after the water jump, with Aeschylus just trailing and Wagner still bringing up the distant rear. Suddenly, over a hurdle, Wagner had somehow snuggled into position between the Greek and Elizabethan giants and before the ink had dried so to speak he was a nose in front and quickly half a lap. Rounding the bend and into the home straight there was only Wagner to be seen …

(Aeschylus and Shakespeare, according to Heinrich Porges the only two dramatic poets who can be considered as Wagner's equals, pay their respects to the master.)
Lebrecht Music & Arts.

The imperfect Wagnerite

The imperfect Wagnerite is thin
on discography and has been known
to yawn during *Parsifal*, has never
flown multiple kilometres just
to catch a performance of *Die Feen*
or *Das Liebesverbot,* has never read
George Bernard Shaw on the subject,
has had some sympathy for Rodney
Milnes, but still revisits the Green
Hill despite finding some of the sights
and sounds disappointing, has a sneaky
liking for *Tannhäuser* for all its faults,
doesn't have an icon of the Master
lording it above the bed, is forgiving
if Siegfried runs out of puff, isn't fluent
in German but knows enough to find
the Master's versification at times
amusing, doesn't have instant recall
of every detail of the *Ring* and isn't sure
what it's all about anyway, has paid only
scant attention to Schopenhauer or young
Nietzsche, has fantasies about a Calixto
Bieito production of *Tristan*, has nagging
creepy feelings about the paintings
at Neuschwanstein and the grotto
at Linderhof, has never signed up
for an 'in the footsteps of' tour,
has never heard Hans Hotter live,
or Kirsten Flagstad for that matter.

But for all that,
will never lose the faith!

The jockey club

They rollicked in with their wine
and whistles, demanding a ballet
in time and place to suit
their aristocratic convenience.
Tannhäuser vanished beneath
this ritual cacophony of protest.

It left a composer once more
denied his chance of walking
in state with other deities
of the scented salons of Paris.

Since then members of a new club
have been jockeying for position
at the forefront of venomous barracking.

If it isn't the music they mount
to castigate, or the music's length,
then it's the man, no longer alive
to experience discomfort, on whom
they exercise the whip along
the stretches of the home straight.

Erlösung dem Erlöser

He may have saved the flagging finery
of opera but his own post-mortem future
remains in the balance. Fingers of acid
were always pointing at him and today
the Twittersphere vibrates with chants

of *Hitler's pet*, *Libidinous poseur*,
and *Anti-Semite*, mingling with taunts
of dragging boredom and threats
to eardrums (though he's no match
for the cacophony splashed each day

into uncomplaining headphones). Family
feuding hasn't helped either. Meanwhile,
the faithful in their buzzing coteries talk
largely to themselves (some even having
the gall to compose stanzas of their own

to supplement the damning chorus).
Where is the redeemer, though, to spread
the gospel out with authority from esoteric
corners and self-congratulatory huddles
to the wider pagan world?

The mind of Wagner

His mind is a forbidding structure
now padlocked for eternity,
its tiers presenting blocks of stone
and squares of darkened glass.

We can never penetrate inside
the core to uncover secrets
of transactions that took place,
the myriad intersecting thoughts,

memories, influences, prejudices.
All we have are modest windows
half-opened, teasingly, allowing
a glimpse from time to time into

a harmonic complexity. We can
treasure the products of this mind
that we possess, have access to,
and speculate about unfulfilled

potential, the tissue scarred
by years of dashed dreams
and frustration, regenerated
by springs of hope and opportunity.

But in the end all that we can
say we're left with are simple
questions such as *why* and *how*,
and ultimately *what*.

What's in a motif?

More than greets the ear,
more than can be explicated,
less than the score's notes,
less than the work's totality,
as much as the deconstruction,
as much as the satisfaction,
meeting the conscious head-on,
infiltrating the subconscious,
posing rounded questions,
offering partial answers.

Thread of one mind's web
defying disentanglement.

The dream

I heard the sound
of Wagnerian tubas
in a tumbling dream.
It was like enriched uranium
destined for a warhead
to explode over petty cares
and obliterate them.

It blanketed the energy
of horns and sliding trombones
and followed me into
a cavernous space where
light impelled me to fall
on my knees and touch

the foundations of the universe.

The year 1883

In the year of his death, oxygen
was liquefied for the first time and
Krakatoa erupted. *The Adventures
of Pinocchio* and *Treasure Island* came
to the world's enchanted readership.
Preceding him to a final resting place
was von Flotow, while the life capital
of Karl Marx ran out in the next month.
Manet followed later, then Turgenev,
and the last surviving quagga expired
in a zoo in Amsterdam. No afterlife there.
But these deficits received most rich
compensation through the birthing
of prophetic Kahlil Gibran. Kazantzakis
began his odyssey in life mere days
after Wagner reached his final twilight
and Kafka was shortly to follow suit.
That same year piped in the births
of Bax and Varèse, not to mention
John Maynard Keynes and Mussolini.

But the 13th of February is the day
to remember.

NOTES

Pilgrims' chorus
The words sung by the pilgrims are:
> *Zu dir wall ich, mein Jesus Christ*
> *der du des Pilgers Hoffnung bist!*
> *Gelobt sei, Jungfrau süß und rein!*
> *Der Wallfahrt wolle gnädig sein!*

This can be roughly rendered as:
> To thee I make my pilgrim way, Jesus Christ,
> Thou who art the Pilgrim's hope.
> Be praised, Virgin sweet and pure.
> To our Pilgrimage please be gracious.

Berlin in 2013
Ver.di stands for *Vereinte Dienstleistungsgewerkschaft* (United Services Union), a trade union with headquarters in Berlin. On occasion its members have been called out on strike. The similarity between Ver.di and the name of a certain Italian composer of operas whose bicentenary was also celebrated in 2013 is a happy coincidence.

The English expression 'to cross your fingers' has, in German, an equivalent: 'to press your thumbs'.

The ship of Theseus
Plutarch's *Life of Theseus* provides the earliest surviving record of one version of a paradox of ancient philosophy as to whether an object that has had all its components replaced remains fundamentally the same object. Plutarch's application of the paradox is to the putative ship of the Athenian hero Theseus, which was supposedly preserved and gradually renovated in its entirety over the course of centuries.

Spare a thought for Minna
Wagner had an affair with an admirer, Jessie Laussot, in 1850, even proposing to elope with her to Greece or the Near East. This plan, however, was scotched by Jessie's husband.

Minna's grave is in the Alter Annenfriedhof in Dresden. As it happens, so are the graves of the husband and wife team Ludwig and Malvina Schnorr von Carolsfeld, who sang the roles of Tristan and Isolde in the original four performances in München (Munich) in 1865. Ludwig died shortly afterwards at the age of 29; Malvina lived until 1904.

A dog's life
Robber was the name of the large Newfoundland owned by Wagner and Minna at the time when they fled from Riga in 1839 and sailed on the *Thetis* to London. The stormy voyage provided part of the inspiration for *Der Fliegende Holländer*.

The woman problem
From the time of the first Bayreuth Festival in 1876 until early 1878 Wagner had a romantic fling with Judith, daughter of French writer Théophile Gautier. Judith translated the 'poem' of *Parsifal* into French, which was one of the excuses they used for remaining in contact with each other. When Cosima ultimately found out, that was that!

Poem 5 of the Roman poet Catullus scorns as worthless the gossip of elderly and humourless people about a vibrant love affair.

Mein Leben
This is the (unreliable) autobiography Wagner began to dictate to Cosima in 1865 in München. It gives an account of his life up to the time of his summoning by an agent of King Ludwig II the year before.

Cosima
The 'Brown Book', given to Wagner by Cosima, became the diary he kept from 1865 to 1882.

Trauermusik
This is usually referred to in English as 'Siegfried's Funeral March'.

Wotan's favourite daughter speaks her mind
Wagner wrote the text of the *Ring* in reverse order to that of the final version of events. *Siegfried's Tod*, written first, eventually became *Götterdämmerung* and *Der Junge Siegfried* simply *Siegfried*. Wagner had particular problems with the ending of *Götterdämmerung* and changed it several times. An originally optimistic ending, especially for the future of the gods, became

much less so, under the influence of Wagner's reading of the philosophers Feuerbach and Schopenhauer. The final version is basically 'Feuerbachian', though stripped of a specific Feuerbachian message at the end. The 'Schopenhauerian' ending had earlier been dropped and was never set to music.

Brünnhilde's imagined words of greeting to her father could be translated as 'Thou Glorious One', and the words towards the end of the poem can be translated as 'Deepest suffering of sorrowing love opened my eyes. I saw the world end.'

Hier gilt's der Kunst
These words from *Die Meistersinger* signify 'Here it's art that really matters.'

The man with the blue gavotte
The reference is to the 1937 work by Wallace Stevens entitled 'The Man with the Blue Guitar'. This is a poem of 33 cantos, a lengthy exploration of art, performance and imagination.

Hunting horns
Frau Minne is a personification of Love.

Dresden Amen
Wagner tells us in *Mein Leben* that during the 1849 revolution in Dresden he climbed the bell tower of the Kreuzkirche to act as a lookout and report on troop movements below.

August Röckel and Mikhail Bakunin both took part in the Dresden revolution and served prison sentences after their capture. The former, a zealous republican and good friend of Wagner, had been his musical assistant for some years at the Court Theatre in Dresden. The latter was an influential Russian anarchist.

Richard and Queen Victoria
Wagner conducted a series of concerts in London in 1855. Queen Victoria attended one of them and spoke to Wagner personally during the intermission. She later recorded her impressions of the meeting in her diary, while Wagner wrote about it in a letter to Minna.

King Ludwig II
The king died in mysterious circumstances at Lake Starnberg, shortly after moves were made to depose him. He had been taken into custody and transported from Neuschwanstein to Berg Castle on the shores of the lake.

Wagner went to some lengths initially to conceal his relationship with Cosima from the king.

A tale of two cities
Venezia: Venice, München: Munich.

Wagner worked on Act II of *Tristan und Isolde* in 1858 during one of his visits to Venice.

Isolde, the first child of Wagner and Cosima, was born while Cosima was still married to von Bülow. The soprano Malvina Schnorr von Carolsfeld, who was first to sing the part of Isolde, had throat problems before the première in München, so that it had to be postponed.

One report has it that Wagner and Cosima had a row on the morning he died, the cause being his supposed involvement with the English soprano Carrie Pringle who had been one of the flower maidens in the performances of *Parsifal* at Bayreuth in the previous year.

What might have been
The references are to some of the works Wagner is known to have contemplated composing at various stages of his career, making minimal or more extensive sketches (mainly of the storyline), but never completing.

The millionaire question
The 1956 film *High Society* starred Bing Crosby, Grace Kelly and Frank Sinatra, who sings 'Who wants to be a millionaire?' The answer to the repeated question is always 'I don't', one of the disadvantages of great wealth being the expectation of owning an opera house box and having 'to sleep through Wagner at the Met'.

More than a facelift
Five years after Eberlein's statue was unveiled, the Prussian court painter Anton von Werner portrayed the occasion; his painting currently hangs in the Berlinische Galerie in Berlin.

When the statue was renovated, the marble needed to repair damage came from the same quarry in Athens that provided the original marble.

Once in Bayreuth
The beautiful Markgräfliches Opernhaus (Margravial Opera House), one of the factors attracting Wagner to Bayreuth in the first place, was next door to the town synagogue. When the Nazis were burning synagogues, the one in Bayreuth was saved from fire because it was feared that setting it alight could cause the opera house to catch fire as well. The synagogue's interior, however, was desecrated.

What value an opera?
Nothilfe means 'emergency assistance' and the surcharge on such stamps generally went to charitable organisations. The first German stamps of this kind were issued in 1923 to help victims of the Rhine-Ruhr floods that year, and there was an issue each year after that. The issue of 1933, the first for the Third Reich, was therefore also the tenth anniversary of the practice.

The imperfect Wagnerite
George Bernard Shaw's idiosyncratic appraisal of the *Ring* cycle, *The Perfect Wagnerite*, was published in 1898.

Legendary opera critic Rodney Milnes died in 2015. One of his many contributions to *Opera* magazine was entitled 'An Imperfect Wagnerite' (June 2011). Somewhat ambivalent about Wagner at the best of times (he did appreciate much of the music if, in his view, it was performed appropriately), he vowed never to return to Bayreuth after slamming performances there in 1988.

Calixto Bieito is a Catalan director famous for his 'scandalous' productions of a range of operas.

Erlösung dem Erlöser
These are the final words of *Parsifal* and mean 'redemption for the redeemer'.